Acting Edition

Two One-Act Plays

100 Things I Never Said to You

100 Love Letters I Never Sent

by Adam Szymkowicz

SAMUEL FRENCH

Copyright © 2023 by Adam Szymkowicz
All Rights Reserved

TWO ONE-ACT PLAYS is fully protected under the copyright laws of the United States of America, the British Commonwealth, including Canada, and all member countries of the Berne Convention for the Protection of Literary and Artistic Works, the Universal Copyright Convention, and/or the World Trade Organization conforming to the Agreement on Trade Related Aspects of Intellectual Property Rights. All rights, including professional and amateur stage productions, recitation, lecturing, public reading, motion picture, radio broadcasting, television, online/digital production, and the rights of translation into foreign languages are strictly reserved.

ISBN 978-0-573-71033-9

www.concordtheatricals.com
www.concordtheatricals.co.uk

FOR PRODUCTION INQUIRIES

UNITED STATES AND CANADA
info@concordtheatricals.com
1-866-979-0447

UNITED KINGDOM AND EUROPE
licensing@concordtheatricals.co.uk
020-7054-7298

Each title is subject to availability from Concord Theatricals Corp., depending upon country of performance. Please be aware that *TWO ONE-ACT PLAYS* may not be licensed by Concord Theatricals Corp. in your territory. Professional and amateur producers should contact the nearest Concord Theatricals Corp. office or licensing partner to verify availability.

CAUTION: Professional and amateur producers are hereby warned that *TWO ONE-ACT PLAYS* is subject to a licensing fee. The purchase, renting, lending or use of this book does not constitute a license to perform this title(s), which license must be obtained from Concord Theatricals Corp. prior to any performance. Performance of this title(s) without a license is a violation of federal law and may subject the producer and/or presenter of such performances to civil penalties. Both amateurs and professionals considering a production are strongly advised to apply to the appropriate agent before starting rehearsals, advertising, or booking a theatre. A licensing fee must be paid whether the title(s) is presented for charity or gain and whether or not admission is charged. Professional/Stock licensing fees are quoted upon application to Concord Theatricals Corp.

This work is published by Samuel French, an imprint of Concord Theatricals Corp.

No one shall make any changes in this title(s) for the purpose of production. No part of this book may be reproduced, stored in a retrieval system, scanned, uploaded, or transmitted in any form, by any means, now known or yet to be invented, including mechanical, electronic, digital, photocopying, recording, videotaping, or otherwise, without the prior written permission of the publisher. No one shall share this title(s), or any part of this title(s), through any social media or file hosting websites.

For all inquiries regarding motion picture, television, online/digital and other media rights, please contact Concord Theatricals Corp.

MUSIC AND THIRD-PARTY MATERIALS USE NOTE

Licensees are solely responsible for obtaining formal written permission from copyright owners to use copyrighted music and/or other copyrighted third-party materials (e.g., artworks, logos) in the performance of this play and are strongly cautioned to do so. If no such permission is obtained by the licensee, then the licensee must use only original music and materials that the licensee owns and controls. Licensees are solely responsible and liable for clearances of all third-party copyrighted materials, including without limitation music, and shall indemnify the copyright owners of the play(s) and their licensing agent, Concord Theatricals Corp., against any costs, expenses, losses and liabilities arising from the use of such copyrighted third-party materials by licensees. For music, please contact the appropriate music licensing authority in your territory for the rights to any incidental music.

IMPORTANT BILLING AND CREDIT REQUIREMENTS

If you have obtained performance rights to this title, please refer to your licensing agreement for important billing and credit requirements.

100 Things
I Never Said to You

100 THINGS I NEVER SAID TO YOU premiered at Lion's Gate Theater at the Willow School in New Orleans on May 5, 2022, with lights by Shawn McCrea and sound & direction by Beau Bratcher. The cast was as follows:

ACTOR . . . . Aniya Fields

ACTOR . . . . Agnes Kilroy

ACTOR . . . . Alex Macneill

ACTOR . . . . Henry Mikulencak

ACTOR . . . . Ronan Newberry

CHARACTERS

Four to one hundred and six high school-age students of any gender.

SETTING

A high school assembly where students stand up and speak.

TIME

Now or when the play is published in case I accidentally date it.

AUTHOR'S NOTE

If you need to make cuts to make it fit a certain time limit, you may do that. Try not to cut interstitials because they help break up the monologue format. You could just not do numbers, omitting both the numbers and the text, or you could say "omitted" after the number.

You are also welcome to change gender of the speaker if it says "she" and you want it to say "he" or "they." Or, for example, change "Waitress" to "Waiter."

Special thanks in no particular order to:

Beau Bratcher and everyone at Willow.

John and Rhoda Szymkowicz, Seth Glewen, the Gersh Agency, Maggie Toole, Tricia O'Toole, Tish Dace, Kristen Palmer, Wallace Szymkowicz. Elizabeth Bochain. Joe Kraemer.

At Juilliard, Tanya Barfield, David Lindsey-Abaire, Stephen Brown, Daniella De Jesús, Lia Romeo, Nick Kaidoo, Jake Brasch, Yilong Liu, Nia Akilah Robinson, Jordan Ramirez Puckett. Evan Yionoulis, Derrick Sanders, Richard Feldman, Kathy Hood, Jerry Shafnisky, Kaitlin Springston, James Gregg, Lindsey Alexander, Hannah Rubenstein, Aly Homminga, Laila Perlman, Jenny Lord.

Sasha Bratt and his students at Naugatuck Valley Community College: Makayla Balducci, Brianna Mattingly, Camila Paredes, Jalon Copeland, Molly Riley.

Amy Rose Marsh, Garrett Anderson, Nate Netzley, Abbie Van Nostrand, Nicole Matte, David Geer, Faith Amrapali Williams, Rebecca Schlossberg, Courtney Kochuba, Rosemary Bucher, and everyone at Concord Theatricals and Samuel French.

Gwydion Suilebhan, the New Play Exchange, and those who left reviews there of this play: Emily McClain, Robyn Ginsburg Braverman, Julia Everitt, Emma Goldman-Sherman, Aly Kantor, Glenn Morehouse Olson, Claudia Haas, Cheryl Bear.

For all those we have lost but especially for
Marnie Schulenburg
Andrew Leynse
Mary Kay Fyda-Mar
Franklin S. Gross
Eunice McNeil
Angus Bailey
Jim Houghton

(This is a play for a minimum of four people, a maximum of a hundred and six. But you probably don't want a hundred and six. I mean, how hard would the logistics be of rehearsing with a hundred and six people? However you break it up, please say all the numbers. The actor can say the number before their part or someone else could say it. Someone could be the "say all the numbers person" if you want. Also someone should say the title to start the play.)

(The text:)

One hundred things I never said to you.

One.

When you died, I cried even though –

Two.

I never liked you much.

Three.

I miss you of course.

Four.

But still.

Five.

That doesn't mean. Don't get the wrong idea. That doesn't mean you were special.

Six.

Of course you were special.

Seven.

This is a school assembly to talk about our feelings about Julie's death. All feelings are valid, except if, okay...All feelings are valid.

Eight.

It was my idea to say out loud the things we maybe never said while Julie was alive...Because. I don't know why. Because we should. We should say the true things we don't say. Don't you think?

Nine.

Julie was complicated and charismatic. Julie was everything, too much, not enough, too young, too old, she wore lots of – well you know. I wish we didn't have to do this. If she was alive, we could just obsess about her quietly in small groups but – Julie was unique. I mean everyone is unique. I know that. But some people are more unique than others and Julie was. The world is a lot less now that she's gone and I mean that in the most visceral way. It's like there's nothing really to talk about anymore or care about or look forward to and that's not all because of her being gone but sometimes it feels that way. Also I think she stole my cat.

Ten.

Julie. Thank you for being in my life. No really. Maybe you had no choice in the matter. Sometimes I glom onto people. Maybe I did that to you. Maybe you were like "get them away from me" and I was all like "hey everybody what's going on?" Sometimes I feel like that's what's happening. I hope that wasn't true. You didn't make me feel that way in any case. I felt like I belonged, like as much as I feel like I can belong, but now that you're gone it's hard to still feel that way. I just wish...no never mind. Sometimes I get so caught up in myself I forget. So, anyway, thank you for letting me be near you, I guess and for being nice to me sometimes and for that one time you told me you admired me. That meant a lot. Even if it was a lie. Was it? Even if it was.

Eleven.

Once we were sitting on the grass, just me and her and she was like "I need to tell you something" and I was like "uh-oh" you know because I didn't know what it was but I got nervous about it anyway like bees in my stomach or something and her face was so serious and I was thinking "why do I even care" except that I did care a lot even if I didn't want to or if I wanted to pretend like I didn't care at all. And then she told me and it was nothing. Just some stupid life thing and I was like why did I get so nervous right then? What did I think she was going to say and why was I worried it was going to crack my whole world open and then she went and died and that cracked my whole world anyway.

Twelve.

It was a car accident. It wasn't anything else.

Thirteen.

You've heard probably the rumors, that she was working to overthrow the government, that she was a spy, that she was a drug dealer, that she was powerful and that power is threatened by power. The last one I think is true. People say maybe it was an assassination by the government and look I don't trust the government as much as anyone but no, it wasn't that. And it wasn't murder. You know deep down if you search your heart, you know that. There was something inside her that she couldn't control and it overwhelmed her and people tried to help and of course sometimes they could until they couldn't. And it's hard for everyone when the person they know who is most alive kills herself but that's what happened and it sucks. It's just so awful.

Fourteen.

She's missing everything.

Fifteen.

You're not missing anything.

Sixteen.

I never said, "Will you marry me." I never said, "Let's run off together." I wanted to say that to you. Every day I looked at you and that's what ran through my head. Maybe I was scared that you'd say no or maybe I was scared you'd say yes. You had that smile. It hurt me. Split me right open even. And when you'd look at me, I mean really look at me – Why did you leave me here? I can't go on. It's too hard without you here. And it was hard with you here too. You were difficult. And you were beautiful. Sometimes you were mean and awful. But also I loved you and I never told you. And now you're gone. And I never kissed you once. So I guess I'm the idiot.

Seventeen.

You were my only real friend.

Eighteen.

I didn't love you. There. I said it.

Nineteen.

I guess you could say you were my nemesis.

　　　(Interstitial.)

A. Hey.

B. What do you want?

A. I'm just checking in. Seeing how you're doing.

B. I'm fine.

A. Did you shower today?

B. What?

A. Did you –

B. I don't know. Maybe. I'm shower adjacent for sure. Like yesterday. Or the day – Stop asking me things.

A. I'm just checking in. Trauma can be –

B. Don't talk about trauma.

A. Trauma can be traumatic.

B. I got to go.

A. But are you…?

B. I'm fine. I'm fine. I'M FINE!!!!!

Twenty.

I never told you what you meant to me. I'm still not sure actually what you meant to me. I looked up to you of course. And you were always there, so there's that. I coveted your clothing. I wanted to be you. I mean, not now. And anyway, did you want to hear that really? That I wanted to be you? Better I think to never say something like that. Not just because it's embarrassing to me but because it's embarrassing to you too. But maybe I should have told you. If only I could have been born as you, maybe my life would be worth something. Don't look at me like that. I know I have low self-esteem. I'm working on it. You were so much more than the rest of us though, weren't you?

Twenty-one.

We crave stories. Good stories, bad stories, funny stories, tragic stories, scary stories, happy stories, sad stories, new stories, old stories, stories we've heard before, new parts in old stories, old parts in new stories…stories with a girl in them. I guess some people don't care about that so much. But I do. And the story is who she was and what she did and said and looked like and that may not seem like enough but we all just live our lives, right?

Twenty-two.

Listen sheeple, she was good with computers and she was up to some heavy stuff and they couldn't let her keep doing that so they took her out. You know that and I know that and I'm not going to say any more so the feds don't come after me too.

Twenty-three.

Please stop. It was an accident. Everyone knows it was an accident. It wasn't murder. She didn't kill herself. It was one of those things. People think a deity wouldn't allow someone to die so young or that there's a reason for it. But we live in chaos and there's no reason for anything and everybody just needs to get used to that. Things aren't going to just start making sense.

Twenty-four.

A car accident is sometimes suicide. You may say carelessness but I say she wasn't happy.

Twenty-five.

Wasn't she happy? She was happy. Are any of us happy? Am I happy? You mean she was clinically depressed? Was she? If so, who else is? What can we do? What do I do? There's help, right? I think there's help.

Twenty-six.

Twenty-five times I tried to tell you what you meant to me but I couldn't.
Twenty-four times I brought you coffee.
Twenty-three times I read to you.
Twenty-two times you read to me.
Twenty-one times you gave me a ride.
Twenty times I asked you what time it was.
Nineteen times I was angry at you.
Eighteen times I asked about your mother.
Seventeen times I played that song you like.

Sixteen times I stopped myself from saying something mean to you.
Fifteen times you wore my jacket before I asked for it back.
Fourteen times I was afraid of what you would say.
Thirteen times I gave you a pencil.
Twelve times I let you copy my homework.
Eleven times I forgot what I was going to say.
Ten times I said the wrong thing and you told me so.
Nine times I celebrated your birthday with you.
Eight times you called me your best friend.
Seven times you told me to go. "Just go."
Six times we danced to my favorite song.
Five times you asked about my brother.
Four times I lent you money.
Three times you used my phone.
Twice you told me to shut up.
Once I spilled soup on you.
Eight hundred and forty-three times you smiled at me.
I kept track.
I have a lot more but I'll stop there.

Twenty-seven.

I was more creative around Julie like I would have new thoughts and ideas and pictures in my head like a lot more than when I was alone. I don't want to say she was my muse exactly but also she wasn't not my muse. I just wonder if I'll be able to make anything now.

Twenty-eight.

In autumn
under blue sky
we jumped in leaves

piles made by old men
and left there.

In winter we balled up ice
and threw it at our friends.

Someone got hurt.
Someone got hurt feelings.

Spring came and we ran and ran
around the track
until we couldn't run anymore
and fell in a heap
of sweaty track and field
teammates.

In summer
we went to the place
where we all
were afraid to
dive in
and we dared each other.

Someone would jump
we knew
if we showed up in our swimsuits
if we waited and dared.

We looked for you there.
you would jump we knew

but you were already gone.

Twenty-nine.

You really made me feel bad about myself a lot. Like I felt ugly around you and stupid. I felt like I couldn't do anything right. I sure couldn't run as fast as you could or speak French half as well. I couldn't make anyone swoon the way you could. And the way you dressed! I tried sometimes to do the thing you did where you roll up your sleeve but it never worked. Or the thing you did sometimes with barrettes? But no. I just looked like I was trying too hard. There was just something about you that just made me want to open myself up with my fingernails and jump out of my skin. Let's just say I always felt bad about myself with you in the world, and now, I should feel better, right? But I don't. Not even a little.

Thirty.

I would always make hardboiled eggs and bring them to school, you know for lunch and I always brought one for you. Nobody liked those eggs like you did. You didn't even care what people thought, because you know, the smell, and everything. The whole eating process. I never cared what people said about me. But I was surprised you felt the same way. I don't think we had a lot in common. But it was nice of you to sit with me every day and eat eggs while everyone watched.

Thirty-one.

We were next-door neighbors and once I remember my parents were away. They're not – well most of you know. My home life isn't – Anyway I was alone and I was little and it was thundering and lightning in a really terrifying way. Flash! Right next to the house and then Boom! I was afraid. I was just hiding under the bed whimpering. And then she was there. And she said, "Are you okay?" She wasn't much older than me. She was probably scared too but she was there to check on me. I came out and we ate some cookies she brought and when the power was out we read to each other under blankets with our flashlights until the storm was over. I'll never forget that. She was – well you know.

Thirty-two.

I spent a lot of time finding just the right mix of flowers to bring to your grave. I wanted to find the ones that you would think were beautiful. I thought about the colors you wore and about your general disposition. I thought about your smell. And look, sometimes the wrong flowers together don't smell right. So I really worked on this. The florist was very annoyed. But I had it finally. A perfect blend that seems like you and that you would like. And I deposited it perfectly on your grave. It was like a spot was saved for me in front. But you weren't there. It was just some grass and a rock. So

I took the flowers back to my car and I drove around trying to think of where to put them. I went to the coffee shop. I hung outside your house. I went to the lake. I went to your old job. But nothing seemed right. So I brought them home. I will watch them die and I will hang them upside down and dry them and I will remember you maybe. I wish I could give them to you but this will just have to do.

Thirty-three.

I'm not gonna talk about her. Everyone else wants to talk about her and I get that but I'm not going to talk about her so put that in your pipe and smoke it. How do you like them apples? Now the shoe is on the other foot. Now we'll see why the chicken crossed the street. All the chickens have come home to roost and the cows have come home so don't serve me no old milk. I'm not gonna drink it. Yeah. Right. Yeah. I don't have much to say anyway. Nothing that hasn't already been said. She was – I'm not going to talk about her. So let the parade just pass by. Anyway, she didn't like me I don't think. So I have no dog in this fight. So get back on your horse and get out of town. Hitch a ride on the first thing smoking and do your due diligence. Anyway, I betrayed her deeply and you know what she did? You know what she did? She forgave me. So. I'm not gonna pay the piper. I won't drink this punch. Sit down old man, this party is just starting. Don't cry me a river. I'm a statue. I'm a – I wish she wasn't so nice to me. I am a rock. I am indelible. I have to – I'm going to sit down.

Thirty-four.

Once we were at a party. And she looked at me.

Thirty-five.

I can't tell this story now. I'm sorry. Someone else go. Okay, I'll say something else. She liked letters. Like getting and receiving notes on actual pieces of paper. That's something.

(Interstitial.)

A. You going to the funeral?

B. No. You going?

A. No.

B. I feel like I should.

A. Yeah.

B. But I'm not going to.

A. Me either.

B. They say closure, right? Like to say goodbye or something. But I think I said goodbye a long time ago.

A. Okay. I just don't like crowds.

B. And I don't want to.

A. And I don't like emotions.

B. Yeah. Okay. I feel guilty though.

A. Yeah.

B. But I'm still not going to go.

Thirty-six.

This is just a blip, right when you think about it, not just in the life of our planet, right? But even in my life. Five years from now, what will I remember. Ten years? Twenty years. I'll forget most of your names. I already forgot your name.

Thirty-seven.

You were the one that made the day bearable and now, I don't know how I will go on.

Thirty-eight.

I've had a lot of people in my life die. This is the same and different. Can we skip the crying this time and just go to the part where we laugh about old times?

Thirty-nine.

People act like there's a mystery to solve. There's no mystery. Everybody dies! Everybody! What did you think was going to happen?! Now I'm shouting! Sorry. Sorry about that. Sorry!

Forty.

We went fishing once on my daddy's boat. I didn't know what it was but the fish didn't like her. Everyone else was doing pretty well. Bass, salmon, eels even but nothing was biting for her. Finally we figured out she never put anything on her hook. She just couldn't do it. For some reason that enraged me. Look I know she was all y'all's friend but I just...she wasn't okay. And it's not just the fishing. Well, you know. You all already know. Sometimes I get angry when everybody says how amazing she was. I know. This isn't the time to say this. I'm gonna go. I'm gonna go.

Forty-one.

This is what I imagine death to be like. You're floating, suspended, but you're also underwater and your body doesn't weigh anything and you can't really feel it. And you can't see anything. It's black. Like black ink or like really dark blue ink. It could be that. But that's all you see. And everything is just silent and you float and you're kind of aware of everything but thinking about it all doesn't hurt or cause you distress. You're free maybe. But also you're not anything. And that's it. You float and exist but don't exist and that's what it is forever. That's death. Some days I look forward to that. But it may not be like that at all so maybe not.

Forty-two.

When you think about it, one person's death doesn't mean all that much, even hers. When you think about it. Life is fleeting. They say that. What else do they say? Life is short? Eat your peas. Make the world better for those who will follow. Tip your server. Um. Make every moment count. Be kind. Don't let them get you down. Use the force, Luke. Stuff like that. Um. Everything is hard, right? Don't make it harder for someone. Um. Use a napkin. I'm sorry. I don't have anything to say. I just think stop being so awful please. It will come back at you. I know you're in pain but it's not the way forward. Really. It's not. Um. Live long and prosper.

Forty-three.

I feel like I'm making this about me. In my head, everything is about me all the time but this right now, this doesn't have to be about me, right?

Forty-four.

What's that? Hold on. I'll be right back.

Forty-five.

I get that it's awful. Okay? None of us are okay. That doesn't mean we need to talk about it.

Forty-six.

Where was I? Sorry about that. Maybe someone else should go.

Forty-seven.

I've been looking at a lot of boats for sale. I can't afford a boat but sometimes I just wish I could go out in the middle of the ocean and be all alone for a while. I used to dream of buying a boat and taking Julie with me.

Forty-eight.

Things you should know about Julie. Her mother was an Olympic gymnast who won a silver once on a beam or something. She also may have been a spy. Or at least that's what people said. Like she was CIA or something maybe. Her father was in insurance, so you know, maybe also worked for the government. FBI or one of those ones we never hear about because they're too secret. They were incredibly wealthy but also maybe they lost it all like ten years ago in like an oil crash or something. Or like a silver mine collapsed or they lost their jobs or something. In any case, at their house there was always the faint smell of disappointment underneath everything. I went there a couple times after practice and had a yogurt. So. It smelled like disappointment and also yogurt.

Forty-nine.

I'm here representing the Secret Society Of Julie's Secret Admirers. We've disbanded. It's not a secret anymore. In case you weren't privy, we met biweekly and would discuss Julie's finer attributes and who she was and wasn't talking to and we read poems written about her and would tell stories. It was kind of like this except with some hope of someday. Or maybe that was never true either. I was hoping to provide some levity actually but. Sorry. Maybe Freddy will come up and be funny. Freddy? Freddy? Did he leave? Freddy? Freddy? I know you were here before. Hey could you come be funny? Are you here? Freddy. He does this impression of me actually that I never appreciated but I hear it's really funny really. Freddy? You don't have to do that. You could do something else. Freddy! FREDDY?!!!!

Fifty.

Argument against suicide. Part one. I mean. Don't do that! It's permanent. Most of us believe it's permanent.

Fifty-one.

Argument against suicide. Part two. It might be more painful to be dead. You might think it's nothingness but it might just be awful.

Fifty-two.

Argument against suicide. Part three. It gets better.

Fifty-three.

Argument against suicide. Part four. You don't want to be remembered that way.

Fifty-four.

Argument against suicide. Part five. Look you can't argue against suicide. But help is available. I can help you. Other people here can help you. Really. I mean what am I going to do? But…I'll find someone.

(*Interstitial.*)

A. Why are people afraid of death?

B. Are you not afraid of death?

A. I'm not not-afraid. But I wouldn't say fear, no fear isn't the primary thing I feel.

B. Well what's that?

A. Huh?

B. The primary thing you feel. What are you if not afraid of death?

A. Resigned? I'm resigned to it.

B. I hate that. Let's stop talking about – I try not to think about it.

Fifty-five.

But like I've been in love with other people after Julie. I know people assume that no one can compare to her and I guess that's sort of true but also with other people, it's just less intense. Which can be a relief actually.

Fifty-six.

Did I tell you she visited me in the hospital? When I had that head injury. I didn't even know she knew my name. I thought it was a mistake. And maybe it was. She held my hand. You might think I was dreaming but I swear. She was there. It really happened.

Fifty-seven.

She was in my art class. She made this really beautiful – I guess it was like a fish tank kind of musical scene. It was really beautiful and hypnotic. I'm crying a little just thinking about it.

Fifty-eight.

She dated my brother. And you know my brother. He's awful. So I lost all respect for her.

Fifty-nine.

When you're part of a community...No. Let me start over. When you turn seventeen...No. You can't just break all the rules and get away with it. That's what I want to say. You can't just...

Sixty.

I think I'm in love right now and it made me think, did she ever fall in love. Like that would be the saddest thing if she died before she ever fell in love. And then I think of my dad. And I'm not sure he's been in love ever. So. I don't know.

Sixty-one.

I never meant to set fire to her book. It just sort of happened. People think I did that on purpose because I hated her or something. But we got along pretty well. She would say hi to me when she saw me. I don't think she blamed me. Sometimes things around me just catch fire, you know?

Sixty-two.

So we did some stuff we shouldn't have done, definitely and I don't want to get into it but I know that has nothing to do with her death. It was just one of those things.

Sixty-three.

Have you ever seen one of those sea birds dive-bombing the water and coming out with a big old fish? That's what she was like.

Sixty-four.

If we could just stop for a second. I mean I know she's in the ground already but did anyone actually see the body? Is she really – I mean do we know that she's really there? Because she couldn't possibly be gone. I mean, right? I just think someone should check. Could someone check?

Sixty-five.

I know we're here for...but could we talk about something else? Anything? No?

Sixty-six.

I want to. Is there something we could do like magic to bring her back? Reverse time and none of us will remember being here in this room right now or that time can be reversed. Just this once. Please? She would just be here again and we could get on with our lives.

Sixty-seven.

Other people died and there was no assembly. How come – I mean I know why I guess.

Sixty-eight.

She was different.

Sixty-nine.

She was different but also was she? Aren't we all important and loved by God? It seems like an absurd thing to say when I say it out loud but we're all valuable.

Seventy.

I'm sorry I beat up her boyfriend that one time. I'm kind of sorry.

Seventy-one.

Dear Julie,

(This is a letter. I'm going to read a letter.)

Dear Julie,

I'll probably never actually give this letter to you. I won't put it in an envelope and put a stamp on it and put it in the mail. Or hand it to you. You won't ever read it. Unless someday I get brave. Julie, I guess the thing I'm afraid to say is that I'm worried I'll always be alone in this life. And you made me feel a little less alone today. And you probably didn't even know when you smiled at me and talked to me and said something nice about me – you probably didn't even know that it meant what it meant to me. But thank you. Maybe someday I'll give you this note. Maybe.

But now I can't.

Seventy-two.

A story. Once there was a girl who was jealous of Julie.

Seventy-three.

Probably there were quite a few when it comes down to it.

Seventy-four.

But this girl, she set out to destroy Julie. She started rumors. She told her friends abominable lies. And she sowed distrust. She said Julie was talking about them.

Seventy-five.

But the girl, she made a mistake. She was caught in a lie. And the whole house of deception fell down on her head. And Julie rose unscathed. Like a phoenix or an angel.

Seventy-six.

But the really astonishing thing, Julie forgave her. Invited her out with the rest of them for ice cream at – you know the place. And they were friends after that for a while maybe.

(Interstitial.)

A. I'm going to date everyone she's ever dated in the order she dated them. And then I'll know.

B. What will you know?

A. I'll just know, you know?

B. What if they don't want to?

A. Why wouldn't they want to?

Seventy-seven.

Sometimes I write things down because it's hard to remember how it really happened and what I really felt. I was sure I had been betrayed and then I went back and read my journal and yeah I was betrayed but in a different way than I remembered. Sometimes I look back at the person who wrote those words and wonder who they were. So I started writing things I remember about Julie. Her hair. Her time on the four-hundred meter. The way she said "whistle." The way people would turn when she walked down the hall, stumble over their words, avert their gaze even. How much of this will I forget or distort from remembering over and over until her face is just a memory of a memory, or her voice. I can't even remember really.

Seventy-eight.

Everything shouldn't be this hard all the time.

Seventy-nine.

I bought a popsicle and it reminded me of her and then I couldn't remember what her favorite flavor was. In the end, I couldn't eat it. Or I ate some of it and threw the rest away.

Eighty.

Her favorite flavor was cherry.

Eighty-one.

No, grape, I think.

Eighty-two.

Cherry.

Eighty-three.

Strawberry.

Eighty-four.

Look, we're still here. You and me and you and you and we're not her but we're something. We do the best with what we have, with who we are. Right?

Eighty-five.

No one ever asks for my opinion. You want to know what I think? You really want to know what I think? I'm not sure what I think actually. Ask me later. Will you? Will you ask me later?

(Interstitial.)

A. I think she's haunting me.

B. What?

A. Sometimes I hear noises or the toilet just flushes.

B. It's probably a faulty flapper. I could fix that for you.

A. Don't you believe in ghosts?

B. Like actual real ghosts? No. But that doesn't mean I'm not haunted.

Eighty-six.

I used to dig holes and shout into them. There was a summer when things were bad and I did it a lot. Once she saw me and asked me what I was doing. And she didn't tell me I was weird or make fun of me. She dug a hole with me and shouted into it herself. And she was really angry actually.

Eighty-seven.

She was kind. Right? That's part of it. I mean not just beautiful and smart and a great runner and an amazing artist but she made you feel better about yourself somehow, sometimes. That's rare.

Eighty-eight.

I have seen the shrapnel. I have heard the screams. When it wasn't clear what kind of person Julie liked when she first got here. Everyone tried to get her attention all the time. Gifts and texts and love notes and strumming guitars. And then she went and fell for –

Eighty-nine.

Me. Her first something here. It was weird. Real weird and it didn't even last that long really. The way she thought about things. How she would stare off into space. When she would smile but you could see something was bothering her she didn't want to say. I never did find out what it was. She just – well one day we just weren't together anymore. She still said hi sometimes. Called me once or twice. Wrote me a letter last week but I haven't opened it yet. I'm not sure I can ever read it now. It's right here. Someday maybe.

Ninety.

It's hard to remember that we're all just individual people and our lives are all real. There are so many people and not that many people here right now but everyone is real and has big full complicated lives and it's easy to forget I guess.

Ninety-one.

I'm going to name my turtle after her.

Ninety-two.

So.

Ninety-three.

Now I lay you down to rest. The day is done.

Ninety-four.

You were the best.

Ninety-five.

I'm afraid of ghosts so please don't haunt me, okay?

Ninety-six.

Rest in peace.

Ninety-seven.

Rest.

Ninety-eight.

Just rest. I wish I could rest.

Ninety-nine.

Goodbye.

One Hundred.

Goodbye.

...

Am I too late? I wanted to say...I wanted to say... There's nothing to say.

100 Love Letters
I Never Sent

CHARACTERS

A play for four to one hundred and ten people of any age.

AUTHOR'S NOTE

A play about love, for most if not all people. Maybe it's good to perform around Valentine's Day? Or any day, really.

If you need to make cuts to make it fit a certain time limit, you may do that. Try not to cut interstitials because they help break up the monologue format. You could just not do numbers, omitting both the numbers and the text, or you could say "omitted" after the number.

You are also welcome to change gender, if it says "she" and you want it to say "he" or "they." Or, for example, change "Waitress" to "Waiter."

Special thanks to:

Flux Theater Ensemble and all those in Core Work, especially Corinna Schulenburg and Sienna Gonzalez. Reed Yurman, Christine Zagrobelny, Chris Wright, Montseratt "Mozz" Mendez, Fiona Hansen, Justin Woo.

Max Decker and MAD Acting Studio. Yonatan Elkayam, Sabrina Stull, Shashaty, Rick Vo, Kianna Vo, RJ Melgar, Kevin Norman, Isaac Anthony, Preet Kaur, Margo Parker, Jamil Karn, Emma Burnside, Deyshaun Tucker, Julie Dell Phillips, Naomi Parker, Denise Culberth, Katarina Lopes, Chris Nayebeyan, India Rashed, Mayuri Bhandari, Carolyne Weiss, Jackie Mitchell, Elliot West, Timothy Kennedy, Christopher Foster, Joe Corzo, Maleah Goldberg, Gabi Vo.

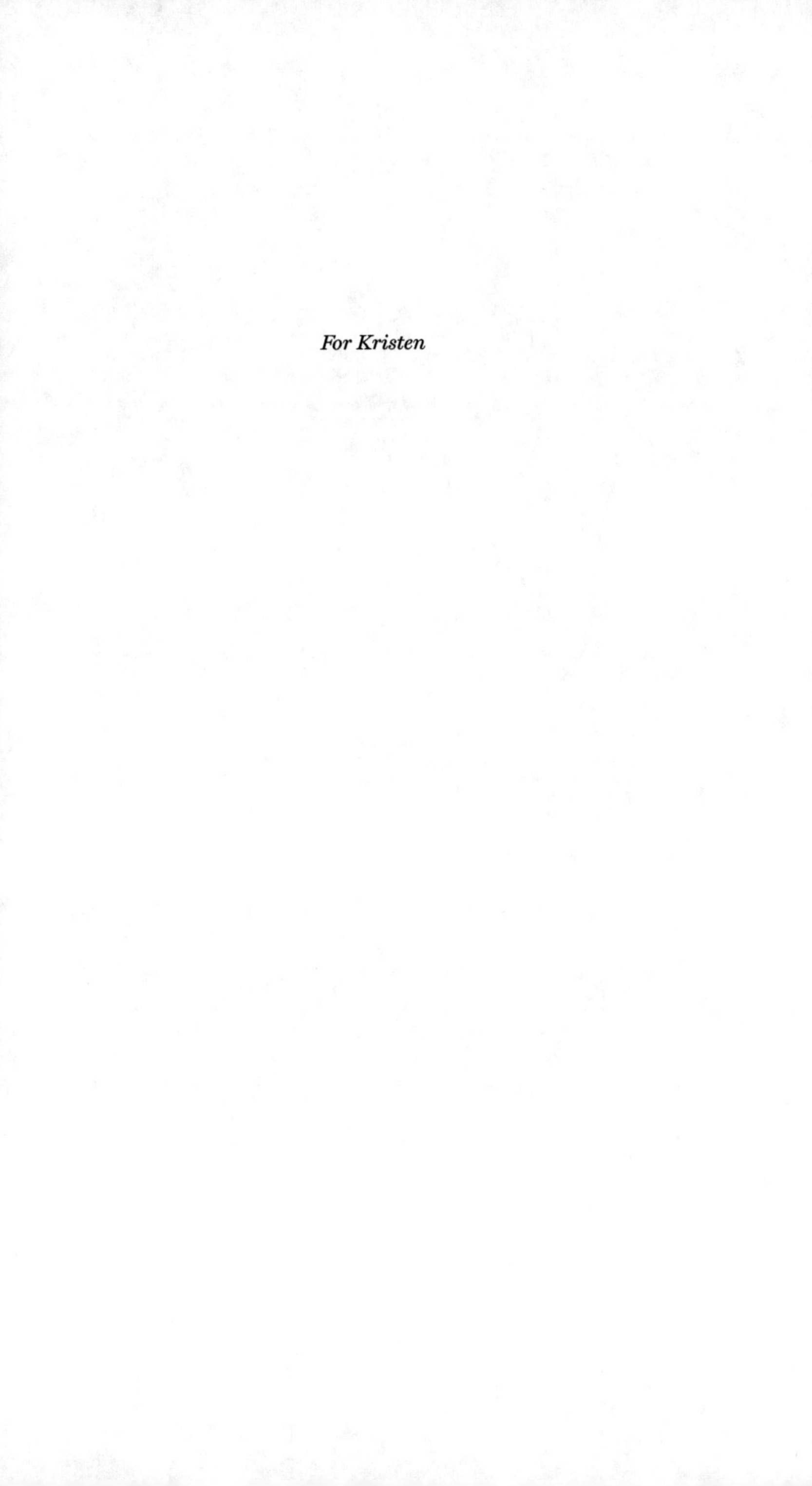

For Kristen

(The text:)

One hundred love letters I never sent.

One.

If you ask me, I'll tell you I find you repugnant but that isn't really true.

Two.

Really it's your eyes.

Three.

Your hands.

Four.

Your body.

Five.

Your face.

Six.

Your feet?

Seven.

You hair.

Eight.

Your eyes. But I know what I see when I look at you isn't what you see when you look at me. So I say nothing. I never say anything. Not when you're sitting next to me. Not when you're across the country. Not when you ask me for advice. Because you look at me and I'm done but I look at you and…nothing.

Nine.

This is not a love letter. You smell bad. You dress bad. You talk too much. You never listen to me. My sister hates you. I wish you would die so I could stop thinking of you. Maybe this is a love letter.

Ten.

What is it about you? Your style? How good you smell? Your smile? I am head over heels for you. I wish you weren't in love with my best friend.

Eleven.

"Look at me! Look at me!" I would write over and over.

Twelve.

Sometimes I go running in the woods to try and forget you.

Thirteen.

But I would write a lust letter. Is that a thing? Or is it just sexting?

Fourteen.

When I first saw you, it wasn't anything. It wasn't love at first sight. You were just one of many. I didn't think much of you. Attractive, sure but nothing special. And I was aware of you. You were around. I was around. We saw each other. And then one day a bunch of us were in the breakroom I remember. And you laughed for the first time and the whole room turned to look at you. And from then on I started to listen to things you said and everyone started to want to be around you. And then one day you wore that hat and it made your eyes pop and that was it. I was gone. And I wasn't the only one.

Fifteen.

You think because you are outrageous, people will like you but it mostly doesn't work that way. I mean it works on me, but not most other people.

Sixteen.

You know what I love about you most? Your kindness. I know that's not a popular thing to say. But time passes and maybe in the end, that's the only thing that matters really. Bad things happen and people go away. Your hopes are crushed, people get sick or someone dies and you're all alone and you're looking around for someone's hand. Just a little bit of decency and when someone offers just a bit of support, or says, "Are you okay?" and means it, well that's a lot more important than I ever thought it would be.

(Interstitial.)

A. You never sent me any love letters.

B. Oh yeah.

A. You said you would.

B. I didn't really think you were serious.

A. It's not too late.

B. Okay. Really?

A. It's not too late.

Seventeen.

I would. But I'm not a poet. And I feel like you only do that when you know what you're doing and I don't know what I'm doing so why embarrass myself, you know?

Eighteen.

I have to tell you how I feel but I'm not going to sign this. You will never know who this is from because I couldn't ever face you after telling you how I feel. I don't know if I know what love is but I know I'd die for you. So that maybe. But also, I may die if you ever find out I'd die for you.

Nineteen.

My biggest problem is you don't say much and what that means is that I project onto you the kind of person I hope you are. I see you thinking and I imagine what you're thinking. You have deep thoughts, I think, about life and our place in it and the purpose of everything. Maybe you have something figured out that we will never understand. But maybe that's not true. Sometimes I see something funny and I want to show you because I think you'll think it's funny too. But maybe you won't. Maybe you're not the person I think you are at all. So this is a love letter for the person I want you to be. And I do want to get to know you. I hope I can. I hope when I talk to you, you'll say things back, more and more. And I'll see what you're really like. And I'll adjust, I think, to how you actually are. I'm sure you'll disappoint me. Everyone does. But that's not your fault. I'm disappointed by myself too.

Twenty.

I pull my beating heart out and give it to you. It's bloody and disgusting and so am I. It's yours. It's all yours. If you'll have it. If you'll have me.

Twenty-one.

I'm ace – asexual but that doesn't mean I don't believe in love. It doesn't mean I don't want to be in a relationship. It just means I go through the world a little differently than most of you do. I don't love you any less.

Twenty-two.

I think about sex all day every day. Sex with you, of course but sex in general and sex with many many others. I don't think this is a problem but also I can't stop so I think I'll just learn to live with being extremely this way. They say someday it dies down. Maybe I won't be like this when I'm old and part of me thinks, cool. I look forward to that and part of me is pretty sure that will never really happen to me. Anyway, this is how I am today. You don't need to know every sexual thought I'm having but you may want to know they are plentiful. But probably you'll forget I'm saying this or think I'm joking. Or it'll make you jealous maybe for a minute and then you'll push it out of your mind.

Twenty-three.

So I bought a typewriter at a thrift store. It was black and shiny and beautiful and it worked. I took it home and polished it until it gleamed and then I put a single sheet in, and turned the platen, I think it's called a platen. And I started to write you a love letter. And I was embarrassed so I stopped. And I put a new sheet in and started over. I wrote about the moon and the stars and your stomach. And that one was bad too. But I tried again. And again. And again. Day after day, I tried. Sometimes for hours, sometimes for only a few minutes. I had to get a new ribbon and learn how to put it in the typewriter. I went through a lot of paper. I learned how to type though I still make a lot of mistakes. For fifty days I tried every day and I never quite wrote what I meant to say. But here is the newest one. No. Wait. Don't read that yet. Let me try again.

Twenty-four.

I don't believe in love. But I guess I could write you a note.

Twenty-five.

I tried to write you a sonnet. But that was hard. Then I wrote a haiku or two. Finally I wrote you a limerick. And then another. I think limericks are actually my form.

There was once a hottie named K.

Twenty-six.

For fifty bucks I will write a love letter for you. Give me a few defining characteristics. A name. Hair color, that stuff. You will not be disappointed. I'm not saying they will fall in love with you, but I stand by my work.

Twenty-seven.

I do believe in love. Maybe someday. Maybe for me. I don't know.

(Interstitial.)

A. What are you doing?

B. I am practicing graceful acceptance for when they say no.

A. You don't know they'll say no.

B. No, I know.

A. They might be into you.

B. Yeah. No. No. It doesn't matter. I never sent it because I don't want to be part of the problem. I don't want to be the one to give unwanted attention.

A. But how do you know? How do any of us know?

B. Sometimes you can tell.

A. Okay but sometimes you can't.

Twenty-eight.

So I wrote twenty letters and sent them to twenty different girls along with flowers for Valentine's Day. I believe it's all a numbers game.

Twenty-nine.

I would take great care of you. Make you meals. Support you and listen to you and get things you need for you. And I know that's kind of what I do, give of myself but for you it would be an act of love.

Thirty.

I want to smash your face in.

Thirty-one.

I know I'm irritating. Sometimes I can't help it. I push you away because I want you to come back. I say mean things. I poke you literally until you can't stand it. I don't want to say these are acts of love but they're kind of acts of love.

Thirty-two.

I've been drawing your face over and over. Sometimes it's from photos and sometimes from memory. You don't look like a model but you're just so...alive. I can't quite capture it but I'm going to keep trying.

Thirty-three.

I made you a mixtape, I mean a mix CD, I mean a playlist. It took me a really long time. I wanted to tell you things and maybe you'll understand when you listen. Will you?

Thirty-four.

I have a life-size cardboard cutout of you in my bedroom.

Thirty-five.

Love isn't creepy. I mean, my love isn't creepy. But maybe if you don't feel the same way, maybe then it's creepy. Sometimes it's hard to know. So I say nothing. I say nothing and pine in silence. I make like a tree and pine. Ha!

Thirty-six.

Sometimes I imagine us as cartoons or anime. I'd be cuter. You're more dangerous. We're both more colorful. Maybe we have swordfights or rob banks. Maybe we should rob banks. I mean not really. Or maybe. Sometimes I think about Bonnie and Clyde but they weren't – maybe they weren't really happy.

Thirty-seven.

I could buy you a puppy.

(Interstital.)

A. Hey.

B. Hey.

A. So I'm breaking up with you.

B. Wait, what?

A. Yeah. You never get me gifts.

B. Well.

A. Or gummy worms. You never show me you were thinking about me.

B. Okay, but I could –

A. You don't look at me like I want you to look at me. You never say nice things or tell me you miss me when I'm not around.

B. No, but –

A. And you never write me love letters.

Thirty-eight.

I was born with an old soul. Which means I'm just grumpy all the time. And don't know how to have fun but sometimes I see how good you are at having fun and I wish that could be me. Maybe you'd reach out your hand and help me have fun. Or maybe I could help you be grumpy and boring with me. Either way. Maybe there's even a middle ground. Or maybe you have better things to do.

Thirty-nine.

I just want to live in the woods like a gnome. Would you come with me and help me construct a gnome house on the side of a hill we could live in?

Forty.

The thing is I don't think love exists. I mean I've never seen it. Have you? I could write you a letter about cake. I believe in cake. So I'm glad to write you a cake letter or a cupcake note. It doesn't mean I won't participate. I'm glad to do all the cuddling and kissing and everything but know that I don't believe there is some eternal higher thing behind it.

Forty-one.

Dear X,

I hate you. I wish I didn't. I wish I wasn't consumed by hate for you. Maybe it would be easier to love you. Maybe then I could love me too. Maybe I could love everybody. But that's not what's happening. What's happening is a deep visceral boiling green hate. I'm so excited for the day I never have to see you again.

All my love,

Y.

Forty-two.

I fell in love with a waitress. What is it about beautiful women bringing you delicious things? I know she didn't make it. I know it's her job and not a sign of her love. But maybe it could be? Maybe I'm different, special. Maybe when she smiles at me it's not just so I'll tip her well. I wonder about her life. I could write her a note and run out before she sees me leave it.

Forty-three.

Just looking for a ride or die. Is that you? Get in touch.

Forty-four.

I can't write you poetry. Or build you a house. Or pay for you every time. I can't find the right words. Or explain anything very well at all. I'm not impressive on a court or out in a field or on a stage. I can't do anything cool. But I think you like me anyway. Do you? I like you too.

Forty-five.

I carry lots of things wherever I go because I never know what you might need. Do you want this chapstick? Do you need a shoelace? A Band-Aid? Aspirin? I have Super Glue. I carry a compass in case we get lost together. I have a bottle of water. I wear this watch in case our phones die. But I also have a power bank to bring them back to life. I have a whistle and a lighter and a flashlight. I have pens and a penknife. A small tent. A sweatshirt you could wear. And a letter I wrote to you so if I ever die you will know I loved you.

Forty-six.

Can I give you a ride?

Forty-seven.

True love I think is actually knowing you and understanding all the annoying things you do and the traps you get stuck in that I can't help unstuck you from. Knowing no one can be everything for everyone. And still being like, yeah. You're the absolute best. You are what I want. And I will be there for you.

Forty-eight.

Or when you sneeze and it's disgusting like everyone is disgusting when they sneeze but I still love you.

Forty-nine.

I work as much as I can because I want to buy you things. I don't even know what things you want really but I will get them for you, even if it take me years, even if it takes me forever.

Fifty.

I bang my head against the wall every day you don't love me until I'm a bloody pulpy mess or unconscious or you say yes.

Fifty-one.

Yes, love is messy. Love with many people is messier. Loving yourself is hard. Not knowing what you want. Not being the person you want to be yet. Messing up over and over. But getting better maybe, a little better every time. You have to just keep trying I think. Or else what's the point?

Fifty-two.

And the seas boiled and the frogs fell from the sky and the earth swallowed the sun and then you looked at me and it all stopped.

Fifty-three.

And I got this record player and I found all the music you love in thrift stores and garage sales and by going to people's basements and to stores even sometimes. So we can listen to it now. We can just be transported separately, together.

Fifty-four.

And I believe in aliens, of course. I mean I don't think you were abducted by an alien like you say you were but I do think it's possible. Sometimes we imagine things until they feel so real we think they actually are real. But our love was never real and you were never abducted by aliens during a concert.

Fifty-five.

But I can do whatever I want. I am not beholden to anything or anyone and yet somehow you have this strange power over me. What is that? How can I get away from that? Tell me how to stop feeling this way. I just want to be free from everything and from you. And yet.

Fifty-six.

Romeo and Juliet were children. They didn't know what love was. Just because you're willing to die if you can't be together, doesn't mean you are actually in love. I blame the easy access to swords and poison and daggers. And feeling trapped. We all feel trapped sometimes in our little lives and it seems like there is a person who is the way out. But a lover will not solve all your problems. Romeo and Juliet clearly show us that. Which is not to say connecting with another person isn't worthwhile. You just shouldn't expect them to save you. Sorry. This is kind of a weird love letter, huh? What I mean to say is, I'm not going to plunge a dagger in my heart but I do love you in my own way, more than a thirteen-year-old from a tragedy could.

Fifty-seven.

Do animals fall in love? Some of them like penguins mate for life. Did the dinosaurs love? When the comet was arching towards them, did they hold each other close with their little arms? Do trees love? I think I love trees.

Fifty-eight.

Dear Z,

I never really had a home because we were always moving, getting evicted. But I feel like you are the home I never had, so...

Fifty-nine.

I believe in science so yeah I think it's all just chemicals and the way some people smell to other people. But that is real and that is what is happening.

Sixty.

It's love when I suggest we carpool. It's love when I come to work and hang out with you even though I'm not on the schedule. It's love when I want to entertain you and be around you. And I'm embarrassed to buy you things so I don't, even though I'm thinking about you. I'm afraid you know I love you but you don't love me back. In fact, I'm almost certain. And I don't want to have that conversation so maybe I'll just stop always being around. I haven't started doing that yet but maybe I'll do that. Soon. Maybe soon. Or maybe I won't. I think love is a problem. For me I mean, love is a problem. I hope that will change someday. This town is too small.

Sixty-one.

I bought a book of famous love letters but it didn't help at all. Because I'm not a famous artist or important person. So I'll just say what I think and hope you like it. I wonder what I think. I think. I think. Let me think.

Sixty-two.

We are stardust. You are a supernova, violently exploding and I'm trying to run around and catch all your pieces.

Sixty-three.

Love will kill us all.

Sixty-four.

I don't want to grow old by myself. I want to be in love and have kids that take care of me. I want to hold hands in the park. And if one of us dies, the other dies a week later from a broken heart.

Sixty-five.

When we write about love, are we writing about trying to fill a hole inside of us with love or are we lamenting the burning hole that love put there?

Sixty-six.

Some people never fall in love, maybe don't even believe it exists. I fall in love twenty times a day. Thirty on weekends. And I don't think my way is better but it's just the way I am. And maybe because I'm dazzled by the humanity in everyone. A laugh or a moment of clarity. A cute cough. Fingers. Hearts beating more rapidly. Your hair. Or other times I'm bowled over when they're not like me, go through life with sharp bones or sharp words. It seems effortless for other people even though I know it isn't. I am a child in a candy store. And I get to see so many people some days. And I know I could love them, so many of them, if they let me. If there was time. But there's never time.

Sixty-seven.

Coup de foudre is what the French say for falling in love at first sight. It means a flash of lightning. It's never happened to me. But I wake up every day hoping.

Sixty-eight.

You bought me cotton candy so I wrote you this letter.

Sixty-nine.

I just want reciprocal love. All my life, my love is unrequited. You never notice me or you make fun of me in the wrong way. Which isn't to say, it's not to say, I haven't been noticed but then I was never interested. Can I just be interested in you and you'll be interested in me too? So I write to you in hopes you can see the good things in me because I know I see the good things in you.

Seventy.

I will win at love! I will conquer. I will defeat!

(Interstital.)

A. How to write a love letter.

B. Who, me?

A. First think of all the things you love about them.

B. Who?

A. The one you love. Then write all the things down in list form. Then write a letter and sprinkle them in.

B. Okay but what's the format? Like a business letter or a cover letter?

A. Forget format. Bleed your heart on the page.

B. But maybe this is for other people to do, not me.

A. It's for everybody.

B. Okay, but not me.

A. Everybody.

Seventy-one.

I want to hold your hand and watch the sunset. It doesn't matter where. Wherever we can see it. A beach, sure or on a bench looking over the river valley. Or just out the window of a motel. Out your windshield. I just want to be where you are. Can we? Will you?

Seventy-two.

You're probably shocked to get a sheet of paper from me on which I've written my feelings about you. Well, strap in buckaroo, it's a wild ride. Part one, in which I describe how you make me sweat and pant and stumble over my words and feel like I'm having a heart attack. My fingers tingle, I hyperventilate, I fall down. I'm writing your full name on the envelope so you don't think it's for someone else. Like your dumb friend or your twin. I know who you are. I can tell you apart.

Seventy-three.

I will never give you the satisfaction of knowing I have feelings for you. You'd really like that, wouldn't you? If I told you I liked you. Well too bad. You are nothing! You are nothing to me!

Seventy-four.

I just want to go back to bed. Never show my face again. Or I could just not ever give you the letter. I'm going to give it to you. But I could just not and then you would never tell me no. And I could have hope a little hope, for a little while, maybe.

Seventy-five.

You are not a light sleeper. So what I'm going to do is, write you a love letter on numbered Post-its which I will stick all over you while you sleep.

Seventy-six.

There will never be an end to my misery. Every day for a year I have written you a letter. I thought, "I'll write it out and I'll find my feelings will change." But it's just gotten worse, every day. So I have this stack of three hundred and sixty-five letters but I think if I were to send it to you or give it to you, you would have an aneurism. So I'll write another one. Just one more, today. Maybe another tomorrow. I don't know. The suffering has to end someday, right? The not knowing? But probably not today.

Seventy-seven.

If I tell you how much I love you, I'm pretty sure I'll never see you again. So I'll just write it down and burn it. No sense scaring you off. We got a good thing. Let's not go into specifics, right? About our feelings. I know you never will. So I'll take your lead.

Seventy-eight.

But the one thing I learned from Julie's death is that it's important to tell each other how we feel now, while we can. So I should tell you…I want to say to you… Sorry, not right now. Maybe tomorrow. Some things are hard.

Seventy-nine.

If I could bring one thing on a deserted island, I would bring you. Or on a rocket ship to outer space. Or in a snow cave. If I had to be trapped in a broken elevator with anyone, it would be you. If I could pick one person to have dinner with or to spend the rest of my life with or to bake a whole lot of cupcakes with, it would be you. Of course. Always. And it's possible maybe there's someone else out there for me or for you. I don't know if I believe in soulmates but I believe in you and I don't know what will happen but I think I might believe in you forever.

Eighty.

I took all the letters I wrote to you and the straw you used and the napkin you wiped your face with that time and that strand of your hair I found on my coat and the ticket stub from when we went to that show together and the mint I saved for you and the stuffed animal I was going to give you and I buried them all. I dug a big hole in the woods and put everything in one by one. I read each letter. I read a poem to the straw. I kissed the strand of hair. And then I filled up the hole again. Let my despair nourish the trees. I don't want it anymore.

Eighty-one.

Or tomatoes. Tomatoes remind me of you too.

Eighty-two.

It's easy to forget everyone you see has a lot going on in their lives. They're fighting battles about time or food or exercise or who they think they should be. Or they have arguments in their head with people who aren't there. Are they still fighting with their mothers? Or their lovers? Are they in love? You, are you in love? Have you ever been in love? I think I might be in love now or at least a sort of psychosis I can only imagine must be what love is.

Eighty-three.

The elf knew she mustn't have these sort of feelings about the goblin. He was, after all, her sworn enemy. But she couldn't bring herself to stab him in the heart as he slept beside her, though it is indeed what she was supposed to do. But what is duty? She watched him sleep, stared at the bugs stuck between his teeth, his rising green stomach. One must have duty to oneself, above all, no? So she did not stab him in the heart that day or the day after or the day after.

Eighty-four.

I'm trying but you're trying...my patience.

Eighty-five.

I know your favorite color, your favorite food, your favorite music, your favorite movie, your favorite team, your favorite flower, your favorite bird, your favorite car, your favorite dessert, your favorite cereal, your favorite drink, your favorite rock, your favorite park, your favorite shoes, your favorite person. But your favorite person's not me. And maybe I never knew you at all.

Eighty-six.

Everyone should get love letters. Everyone should have love letters written to them. Don't be shy. Or scared. Please write the thing you want to say down. And give it to them. You also have to give it to them.

Eighty-seven.

I just don't want to die alone.

Eighty-eight.

When the apocalypse comes, I just want you in my bunker. Also I need you to find a bunker.

Eighty-nine.

When I'm on my deathbed, breathing my last breath, I hope that you will be there, holding my hand. If I don't outlive you. I'll probably outlive you.

Ninety.

I did believe in love before you ruined it.

Ninety-one.

I just want you to hold me.

Ninety-two.

Just love me forever. Is that so much to ask?

Ninety-three.

For me this is a love letter about you and me, for now. Until something better comes along. I think we can both do better. Especially me.

Ninety-four.

I'm not saying every day is good. Or that every moment we have pure love. I'm just saying, you're still the only one for me.

Ninety-five.

And I too rattle at cages I shouldn't rattle at. Which is why I need you.

(Interstitial.)

A. Can we stop the play? Hold on a second. ______, will you come here for a second? I know you hate things like this but I want to say in front of everyone, that you are everything to me and I want to spend my life with you. Can you...will you marry me?

B. Me?

A. Is that a yes?

B. Yes!

Ninety-six.

Oh, wow. That wasn't supposed to happen. Okay. Should we keep going? Your hair is beautiful hair and it's pretty and so are you? Sorry. I can't follow that. Pretend this is a good love letter and that I remembered all my lines.

Ninety-seven.

Or tomatoes. I love the way you say tomatoes.

Ninety-eight.

I don't want to just be friends. I can't just be friends with you. So I need you to change your mind on that. Please. Please.

Ninety-nine.

Should I go? I'll go. This is a love letter to you. You know who you are. Come find me after.

One Hundred.

So I signed it and I gave it to him. And now he has it. And there's a short time of possibility between now and whenever he opens it when anything could still happen.

End of Play

www.ingramcontent.com/pod-product-compliance
Lightning Source LLC
Chambersburg PA
CBHW070402120726
47909CB00008B/2953